ALL ABOUT MAY
May's Big Messy Family!

Written by A. T. Woehling
Illustrated by Felicia Whaley

Ready-to-Read

SIMON SPOTLIGHT

New York London Toronto Sydney New Delhi

For Ms. Chike, and the writer you saw in me.
For my big family—without you, life would be too neat.
Our magic is in our mess.
—A. W.

For Harmonie.
Cherish and embrace the awesome moments along
with the delightfully messy ones
that families create!
—F. W.

SIMON SPOTLIGHT
An imprint of Simon & Schuster Children's Publishing Division
1230 Avenue of the Americas, New York, New York 10020
This Simon Spotlight edition May 2024
Text copyright © 2024 by A. T. Woehling
Illustrations copyright © 2024 by Felicia Whaley
SIMON SPOTLIGHT, READY-TO-READ, and colophon are registered trademarks of Simon & Schuster, LLC.
Simon & Schuster: Celebrating 100 Years of Publishing in 2024
For information about special discounts for bulk purchases, please contact Simon & Schuster Special Sales at
1-866-506-1949 or business@simonandschuster.com.
Manufactured in the United States of America 0324 LAK
2 4 6 8 10 9 7 5 3 1
Library of Congress Cataloging-in-Publication Data
Names: Woehling, A. T., author. | Whaley, Felicia, illustrator.
Title: May's big messy family / by A. T. Woehling ; illustrated by Felicia Whaley.
Description: Simon Spotlight edition. | New York : Simon Spotlight, 2024. | Series: All about May | Audience:
Ages 4 to 6. | Summary: From breakfast to bedtime, May and her seven siblings lovingly run amok and make
a beautiful mess. · Identifiers: LCCN 2023030461 (print) | LCCN 2023030462 (ebook) | ISBN 9781665942843
(paperback) | ISBN 9781665942850 (hardcover) | ISBN 9781665942867 (ebook)
Subjects: CYAC: Stories in rhyme. | Siblings—Fiction. | Family life—Fiction. | LCGFT: Stories in rhyme. |
Picture books. | Readers (Publications) · Classification: LCC PZ8.3.W795 May 2024 (print) | LCC PZ8.3.W795
(ebook) | DDC [E]—dc23 · LC record available at https://lccn.loc.gov/2023030461 · LC ebook record available
at https://lccn.loc.gov/2023030462

My family is a mess.
Yes, a mess!

We wake up too early
and make too much
noise.

Our parents keep pleading, "Go play with your toys!"

So we scoot
and we crawl,
away down the stairs.
No time like the present . .
for musical chairs!

YIKES!
We are just a mess!

Pancakes are stacked,
and the syrup is sticky.
To carry them all
is really quite tricky!

So we slide,
and we slip,
and we shove
toward the table.

Uh-oh . . . we forgot . . . OUR GIGANTIC DOG, MABEL!

SMASH!
We are just a mess!

"It's raining, it's raining!"
we all start to shout.

The timing is perfect,
for Mom wants us out!

So we jump,
and we flip,
and we fly out
the door.

The puddles are HUGE,
so we have a mud war!

THUD!
We are just a mess!

We are off to the tub,
to bathe and get clean.

But that is not really
what happens . . .
if you know
what I mean.

We blow, and we fluff,
and we form
one big bubble.

Dad opens the door . . .
Whoops!
This means trouble!

POP!

We are just a mess!

We march to our rooms,
where our bunk beds
stand tall.

We holler, "Good night!
Good night, one and all."

But . . . we peek,
and we sneak,

and we build
a tall fort.

We read about dragons,
and pizzas,
and tortes!

CRASH!
We are just a mess!

So we gather,
and we pile,
and we snuggle
all as one.

And without a fair warning, the day is quite done.

Wow, we are just a mess.
But this is our mess . . .
and our mess is best!